Welcome to The Giggle Club

The Giggle Club is a collection of picture books made to put a giggle into early reading. There are funny stories about a contrary mouse, a dancing fox, a turtle with a trumpet, a pig with a ball, a hungry monster, a laughing lobster, an elephant who sneezes away the jungle and lots more! Each of these characters is a member of **The Giggle Club**, but anyone can join: just pick up a **Giggle Club** book, read it and get giggling!

Turn to the checklist on the inside back cover and tick off the Giggle Club books you have read.

TEE HEE!

HA HA!

For the cousins – Abby, Amelia,
Andrea, Ellen and Megan
P. R.

To my great-nephews – the twins,
Rupert and Charlie – with love
H. C.

First published 1998 by Walker Books Ltd
87 Vauxhall Walk, London SE11 5HJ

10 9 8 7 6 5 4 3 2

Text © 1998 Phyllis Root
Illustrations © 1998 Helen Craig

This book has been typeset in
Calligraphic Antique.

Printed in Hong Kong

British Library Cataloguing in
Publication Data
A catalogue record for this book is
available from the British Library.

ISBN 0-7445-5497-7

TURNOVER TUESDAY

Phyllis Root

illustrated by
Helen Craig

WALKER BOOKS
AND SUBSIDIARIES
LONDON • BOSTON • SYDNEY

One Tuesday Bonnie Bumble baked **six** plum turnovers for breakfast.

"Delicious," she said,
and she ate up five,
every bite.

There wasn't even a crumb
left over for her little
dog, Spot.

But when Bonnie Bumble got
up from her chair, she turned
over upside down.

And nothing
could turn her
back over again.

So Bonnie Bumble put
her hat on her feet
and her shoes on
her hands.

Then she went
to do her chores.

Upside down she
milked the cow.

But the milk
SPLASHED out
of the bucket.

Upside down she gathered the eggs.

But the eggs SMASHED out of the basket.

On the way back to the house, the sheep nibbled her hair.

And the pig's tail tickled her ear.

"This will never do!"
said Bonnie Bumble.

Back into the kitchen she
went to find the last
plum turnover.

Upside down she ate it,
almost every bite.

When she got up from
the table, she turned
back over,

right

    side

        up!

"Thank goodness everything's back to normal," said Bonnie Bumble.

And it was ...

except for Spot,
who had eaten
up all the crumbs.